# Dear Parent:

Congratulations! Your child is taking the first steps on an exciting journey. The destination? Independent reading!

**STEP INTO READING®** will help your child get there. The program offers five steps to reading success. Each step includes fun stories and colorful art. There are also Step into Reading Sticker Books, Step into Reading Math Readers, Step into Reading Phonics Readers, Step into Reading Write-In Readers, and Step into Reading Phonics Boxed Sets—a complete literacy program with something for every child.

## Learning to Read, Step by Step!

**Ready to Read   Preschool–Kindergarten**
• big type and easy words • rhyme and rhythm • picture clues
For children who know the alphabet and are eager to begin reading.

**Reading with Help   Preschool–Grade 1**
• basic vocabulary • short sentences • simple stories
For children who recognize familiar words and sound out new words with help.

**Reading on Your Own   Grades 1–3**
• engaging characters • easy-to-follow plots • popular topics
For children who are ready to read on their own.

**Reading Paragraphs   Grades 2–3**
• challenging vocabulary • short paragraphs • exciting stories
For newly independent readers who read simple sentences with confidence.

**Ready for Chapters   Grades 2–4**
• chapters • longer paragraphs • full-color art
For children who want to take the plunge into chapter books but still like colorful pictures.

**STEP INTO READING®** is designed to give every child a successful reading experience. The grade levels are only guides. Children can progress through the steps at their own speed, developing confidence in their reading, no matter what their grade.

Remember, a lifetime love of reading starts with a single step!

Visit us on the Web!
StepIntoReading.com
randomhouse.com/kids

Educators and librarians, for a variety of teaching tools, visit us at
RHTeachersLibrarians.com

*Library of Congress Cataloging-in-Publication Data*
Winkelman, Barbara Gaines.
Pinocchio's nose grows / by Barbara Gaines Winkelman ; illustrated by Orlando de la Paz and Paul Lopez.
p. cm. — (Step into reading. A step 2 book)
Summary: Before he can become a real boy, a kindly woodcarver's favorite puppet must learn right from wrong.
ISBN 978-0-7364-1213-1 (trade) — ISBN 978-0-7364-8001-7 (lib. bdg.)
[1. Fairy tales. 2. Puppets—Fiction.]
I. La Paz, Orlando de, ill. II. Lopez, Paul, ill. III. Title. IV. Series: Step into reading. Step 2 book.
PZ8.W7205 Pg 2003 [E]—dc21
2002013359

Printed in the United States of America    10 9 8

# STEP INTO READING®

STEP 2

# DISNEY
# Pinocchio

# Pinocchio's Nose Grows

By Barbara Gaines Winkelman

Illustrated by Orlando de la Paz and Paul Lopez

Random House 🏠 New York

Once there lived
a wood-carver.

The toy he loved most
was a puppet.
He called the puppet
Pinocchio.

One night,
a wishing star
twinkled in the sky.

The wood-carver
made a wish.
He wished that Pinocchio
were a real boy.

A blue light filled
the workshop.
The light turned into
the Blue Fairy!

She waved
her magic wand
over Pinocchio.

Pinocchio opened
his eyes!
"Am I a real boy?"
he asked.

"You may become
a real boy someday,"
said the Blue Fairy.

"But first,
you must learn
right from wrong,"
she said.

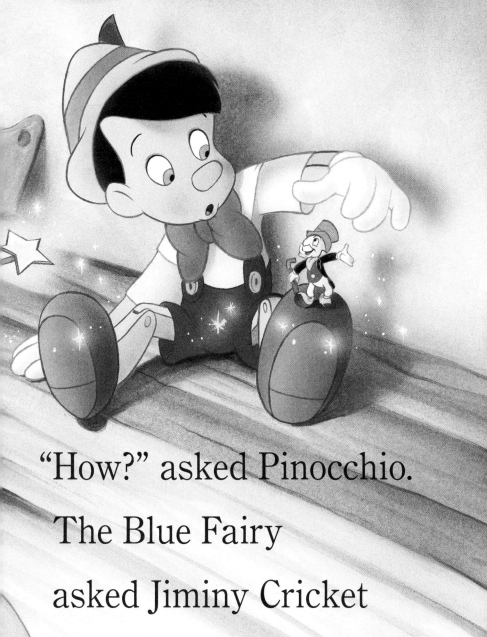

"How?" asked Pinocchio.

The Blue Fairy

asked Jiminy Cricket

to be Pinocchio's helper.

And then she left.

The wood-carver saw
Pinocchio.
He thought his wish
had come true.

He was very happy!

They danced and sang.

The wood-carver sent
Pinocchio off to school.

Pinocchio carried his book

and an apple for the teacher.

A cat and a fox
stopped Pinocchio.

"Come with us,"
the fox said.
"We will make you
a star!"

Jiminy Cricket called,
"Where are you going,
Pinocchio?"

Pinocchio did not listen.

He did not want to go
to school.

He wanted to be a star.

Pinocchio danced

on a stage.

He liked being a star!

But then he was
locked up in a cage.
"Help!" cried Pinocchio.
Jiminy Cricket could not
get Pinocchio out.

The Blue Fairy heard
his cries.
She came at once.

"Why are you not at school?" she asked. Pinocchio was afraid to tell the truth.

So he told a lie.

"Two monsters tied
me in a sack!"

His nose grew and grew!

"A lie is as plain
as the nose
on your face,"
said the Blue Fairy.

Pinocchio shook in fear. "I guess lying is wrong," said Pinocchio. He promised never to lie again.

"Good," the Fairy said.
"You are learning."
She waved
her magic wand.

Pinocchio was free!

His nose was small again.

"Let's go home!"

said Jiminy Cricket.